Voices of Antiquity Encouraging Today

DR. ELIZABETH A. KENNEDY

Barnabas Publishing, PO Box 2316 Ruston, Louisiana 71272
(318) 514-9724
www.barnabasglobal.net

Voices of Antiquity Encouraging Today
Copyright © January 2023 Dr. Elizabeth A Kennedy

First Edition, 2023

Edited By: Dr. Lynda Linn

Cover Photo By: EAK Photos

Hardcover ISBN: 978-0-9913116-3-7
Paperback ISBN:978-0-9913116-2-0
eBook ISBN:978-0-9913116-4-4

Dedication

*F*riends, peers, relatives, strangers, teachers, coworkers, and many others have all contributed to the successful completion of the manuscript that is now this book in front of you. Each has given words of correction, direction, encouragement, insight, caution and the like that was invaluable in bringing the manuscript writing to a final period. First Lady Darlene Wilson, Hawaii Jurisdiction Church of God In Christ was the inspiration that gave birth to the subject matter content. Dr. Lynda Linn, faithful friend and editor, knew just what and when to speak words that brought me back to the writing task when life issues pulled me away. Mentee and friend, Ms Jackie Gilbert's ever-present voice in my mind saying, "You need to write that" nudged me forward when the chorus of "just forget the writing" played the loudest. Dr. Isaac Moore, lifelong friend and battle buddy, helped me to see beyond my limitations to limitless possibilities. Dr. Mary Elizabeth Kennedy my shining star, fierce advocate, and incomparable daughter relentlessly reminded me of the source from which my writing gift came and the purpose for which it was to be used. Most important of all, this book is dedicated to the Giver of life and the lives of those voices that may be transformed through their interaction with the Voices of Antiquity.

Contents

Contempo: Desiring More Receiving Less

Your phone alarm rings at six in the morning instead of the usual seven. You bounce from the bed, feet barely touching floor, and head for the bathroom. You have been scheduled to attend a very important meeting at your company at nine this morning. Your next career move depends upon the outcome of this meeting. The vice-president for Human Resources personally informed you that your productivity was of such excellent character and quality that senior management had arranged this meeting to discuss your future with the company.

That conversation with the VP was two days ago, and since that time it has been almost impossible for you to manage your present assignments. Your mind in overdrive, raced to determine the purpose for this unusual meeting with senior management. The office grapevine had been ripe with all sorts of juicy tidbits about a company shake-up, promotions, demotions, and firings.

Standing before your wardrobe you thoughtfully consider your attire. Competence and professionalism, conservative with a hint of playfulness sent the correct message. Nothing flashy. "That new silk shirt, the one that cost you a week's salary, is perfect" raced through your mind. "Coffee, just one more sip is too much," you hear in your head. Overriding the warning from your mind, you opt for one more cup of coffee.

There it is, your shaking hand spilled the coffee. Your perfect attire is saturated, and your front is on fire from the hot liquid. You catch yourself just before the string of expletives deleted gushes from your lips.

Changing clothes did not interfere with your time schedule with it's allotted time for the little unknowns. The water main break on your usual route and the twenty-minute detour was something that had not factored into the schedule, but traffic was moving and you still had a ten minute cushion. Arriving at the company parking facility five minutes later than your usual time presented a new problem. Spaces at the front of the garage closest to the building entrance and lobby elevators were full forcing a drive to the upper levels. Looking for a space used up another ten minutes of your now gone time cushion. Nine o'clock. You are now still in the garage, and officially late for this most important meeting. It would be a sprint to get to the meeting 10 minutes late. You could do it, if the public elevators to the executive suite were on the first floor. And if they were not filled with people stopping at every floor before sixteen, you could make it by ten after nine. Of course, you arrive at the number two elevator just in time to see the doors close. A quick glance to the right and left. Elevator number one is on floor six going up. Number three is on floor ten going up and number four has a reserved for sixteenth floor personnel only sign.

Just as you turn to enter the sixteenth floor only elevator, your memory says, "Hello, where is the key?" The string of expletive deleted words will not be denied expression. If a mirror were available, you would be able to see the skin color change in unison with the hot blood that was filling the veins in your neck and face.

More people are gathering around you waiting for the elevators to return to the first floor. It is no longer a question of will you be late; rather it is now, just how late will you be? An audible sigh escapes your lips and with it the hopes and great expectations that you held for this meeting.

But survival mode kicks into high gear. Surely you can run up fifteen flights of stairs to make the meeting fifteen minutes late. The stairwell is about twelve feet from where you stand. You can cover the distance in five giant steps. Proud of your accomplishment, you push the stairwell door open.

A bigger than life sign greets you: "Closed for Emergency Repairs. Use the North Corridor Stairs." Determined to deny the mounting sense of doom to rob you of this opportunity, you rush back to the elevators in time to see a smaller group of people. Number three elevator is on the upward journey again. Waiting for the next elevator is the only viable option in front of you. You will your eyes not to look at the world clocks bank above the elevator doors. A mental dare prevents your hand from raising your phone to your face. Twenty minutes late for the scheduled meeting, you stand looking at the sixteenth-floor conference room door. The darkened opaque glass speaks louder than any words. No lights, no sounds from the other side of the door, the room is dark, the meeting over.

Disappointment? Yes. Frustration? Probably. Anger? Possibly. Needing or desiring someone or something to blame? Maybe. The fleeting glimpse of what started out to be the possibility of the biggest promotion of your career just a mere two hours ago flashed across the screen of your mind. Poof. Through no actions on your part, it is gone in a flash. The darkened room tells the story. Upper-level management was here at the appointed time, but you were not. Can it be salvaged? You turn, inhale deeply and command your feet to carry you back to your cubicle two floors below. In that moment you silently instruct your shoulders to rise to an erect posture, gather yourself, put on your "it's not the end of the world" face and head to your office.

The above events did not happen. They are creative license and fictional imagination at work to set the tone for an examination of a construct, Encouraging, in human discourse. Had the events depicted happened in real life, the person experiencing them would have been receptive to someone, anyone, saying or doing anything to make the stinging reality a little less harsh. That is called encouraging.

When encouraging is present, it is readily recognized; and when absent, greatly desired. Chapter 1 begins a series of ten biblically based factual life events foundational to the fictionalized narratives which guide the reader in an examination of encouraging. These stories, pulled from the writer's imagination after prayerful biblical study, are intended to make the reader aware of new and novel ways in which encouraging is operative in our daily lives.

Many of the characters and events chosen have the advantage of being the more obscure and less well known or talked about. Some have one line of scripture to call attention to their presence. Others have nothing that calls attention to their presence. Therefore, the expectation is that there is somewhat less likelihood of the reader coming to the story with preconceived biases or prejudices.

Eve: Groundbreaker and Fountain from Whom all Flow

Hello, my name is Eve. I look forward through the centuries with wonder and amazement. The events, circumstances, words, actions, thoughts, of future centuries as time moves forward to its ultimate conclusion, lay before me as instances of courage, encouragement, and encouraging. You may be aware of my story from the Biblical record, the academic and theological debate, and countless opinions about my role in human history. Although essential to humankind's knowledge and understanding of God the Creator, that is not my story that I'm telling you today. Today I'm telling you about Eve, the first female human being.

I did not exist before the Lord God made me by taking a bone from the man that he had already made. Thinking about that alone is mind blowing; but with all of the knowledge that 21st Century science has produced; it is not too much of a leap. That one bone had everything in it – stem cells– that the human body needs. Those stem cells just need growing and developing time to become the tissue, organs, and systems that make up the human body. The Bible doesn't give the details of how much time went into the making of my body from that one rib bone. It probably is immaterial to what I'm telling you about how I lived my life.

Being first has both its good and not so good points. For instance, I have no history. There is nothing and no one to which I can look back and find an example. I have no parents, siblings, relatives, or friends. I am in the world, which is totally new, alone and left to figure out the process of life and living. Yes, Adam was with me, but he had the same situation. He was without history, parentage, or human companions except me.

I was made fully grown although I didn't know that until after Cain was born. My first try at walking was not very good. I stumbled and had trouble staying with my legs and feet on the ground, and my head pointing up toward the blue overhead. I kept feeling something pulling me forward and downward. I was a fast learner. After the first few days I was able to keep myself with my head pointed up toward the blue in spite of the great pull that I felt. I asked Adam about the pulling downward. He told me that he felt the same thing, but he didn't know what it was. He had learned to ignore the pull. He told me to do the same thing. It wasn't long before I could run through the plants, stoop and hide behind one, until Adam found me. We liked to play that game which we learned by watching the animals. I would run away from Adam and then he would run away from me. We kept that going until the light was gone and we couldn't see each other. When the light was almost gone, we would go to the plant with the big wide leaves and huddle together under it until the light came back.

Adam told me that God called the blue overhead "sky" and under our feet, He called "ground." Those things meant nothing to me, but that's what I started calling them.

God and Adam talked every cycle of the bright light in the sky. They talked until the bright light started going toward the line that I could see behind the plants. The talking would stop just before all of the light was gone. Adam would tell me what to call things. I was very curious and had a what, where, how, when, or why all of the time. Sometimes I would sit with Adam and God as they talked, and God would answer my questions for me.

We did have the animals, and we learned the basic survival skills from watching them. We watched how they huddled together in the rain to keep each other warm, so we did the same thing. Then we figured out that going into the big hole on the side of the hill was better. Rain didn't come into the hole except right at the opening. Adam told me it was a cave.

Adam told me that God said we could eat any of the plants, but not the fruit of the tree in the center of the big space. Adam would eat only a few of the plants. I was much more curious and ate any of the green plants and berries that I found. One day I saw a very shinny smooth berry on a plant that wasn't round like the others, but long and pointed at one end. I pulled it off the plant. It was very easy for me to move my fingers along the long berry from its stem to its tip. A new pleasing sensation went up my nose when I pulled the long berry close. My ears heard a crisp snap as my teeth clamped down on the berry. As soon as my ears heard the snap water began running down my face. Something very bad was happening in my mouth. I threw the long berry down and put both hands in my mouth to stop whatever was happening.

"Water!" I ran to the water spring and splashed cold water on my face and in my mouth. The water made the sensation worse. Later I went to the place where Adam and God talked. God looked at me and smiled. After eating some more of the plants that didn't have great taste, I watched the animals. If the animals ate the plant, I would also eat it.

Although God said that we could eat the plants, He didn't tell us how they would taste or feel. Watching the animals eat and then eating what I saw them eat was a better plan than just trying anything. After I started watching the animals, I ate what they did and had far fewer times of bending over to wait for an explosion to shoot out my backside. Adam and I learned fast.

Adam and I learned to talk to each other by repeating what God said to us. God would make a sound and we'd keep trying until we could make the same sound. God would tell Adam (or both of us, when

I was with them) what the sound meant. Adam had already named all of the animals when God made me, so he told me what to call them. I didn't like being around the large animals who would come to walk with me when I was walking among the plants. They were so large I couldn't see around them. That made it hard for me to find my way back to Adam. One day I followed the animals to the middle of the plants, and then I saw it just standing there.

It was just as Adam had said it would be, alone in an opening with pretty large things hanging from its limbs. I stayed there and watched it for a long time before returning to Adam. I can't remember how many light and dark cycles passed before I went to look at the tree again. I walked closer but I wouldn't touch because Adam said we weren't to eat from that tree. "God said not to eat anything from that tree," Adam told me.

The next time I went to the open space with the tree in the middle, I saw a beautiful new creature standing under the branches. It did not look like any of the other animals that I'd seen. "Hello," it said. I stopped walking unable to move. When my legs would move again, I turned and ran to Adam as fast as I could.

"Adam," I gasped between taking in gulps of air. I told him what I had just seen. "That is the serpent," Adam said before a long pause. Then he said, "I don't know what it wants."

It was a long time, many light and dark cycles, before I went back to the open space with the tree. I always stopped at the opening edge and would not go near the center, even though the serpent kept tell me it was alright to come to him. The serpent didn't look like the other animals. It could talk just as Adam and God talked. I don't know if you've read or heard what happened when I finally walked close enough to talk with the serpent. I'm not going to repeat what we said. I don't think anything I say will change your mind. If you heard the story, you've already formed an opinion, if not it won't change anything. My purpose in telling you my story is for you to get a better understanding of what life was like for me. Let me just say that what happened wasn't good.

Adam and I didn't wait for God in our usual place after our encounter with the serpent and the fruit of the tree. Adam hid because he could see himself. I hid because I could see myself and Adam. He didn't look like the animals, plants, or what he looked like before we ate the fruit. Before we ate, he looked like Adam. Afterward he looked different, unlike anything that I had seen. He had fur like the animals covering his body. Long fur covered the top of his head and around his mouth and nose. He had long dangling things on both sides of his body. He wasn't the same. He had a different look in his eyes, one that I had not seen before, when he turned in my direction. Somehow, I knew everything had changed and would never again be as it was before.

I had no idea how much my life would change, but as I learned of the changes, I felt a new sensation. You would call it fear or terror. Everything that I had learned to that point was useless. I was afraid of the animals, and they seemed to know that things were different. Where they had walked and made me one of them, they now stayed away. And if they came close, I could see a new look on their faces. It was the same look I had seen when one of the larger animals killed a smaller one to eat. I started staying as far away from the animals as I could.

Adam stopped running through the plants with me playing our game of hiding. When he looked at me, there was a different expression on his face. I no longer saw the corners of his mouth turn up at the sight of me. The space on his face above his eyes had creases all the time, and water drops began running down the sides of his face when he was out in the sun. He told me that the bright light in the sky was the sun. Adam stopped being my companion because he was gone during the light looking for berries and plants for us to eat.

When he came back from hunting berries, he wanted to treat me like I had seen the animals treat each other before one of them had a little one. I started accepting that Adam was just being his new and changed self. I started growing around my middle. I kept getting larger until one day I had very bad sensations in my middle section. The sensations came and went. They didn't stay constant, but each one was stronger than the previous. Nothing would stop the strange new sensations. Before when I had sensations like that in my middle from eating new berries and plants, they would go away after I went to the bushes and everything in my middle came out. But this new sensation didn't stop. I tried but couldn't make anything come out of my backside for two whole days (that's what I started calling the light). On the second day just before the sun went behind the trees the pain was so bad, I felt that everything in my middle would come out.

I could barely walk because the sensations were very long and very hard. I made it to one of the bushes that I would lay under when it was dark. I squatted even though it was not dark. I felt a wrenching tearing sensation unlike any other time I needed to get berries out of my middle. Something unimaginably huge was coming out of me. I wanted to move, but my arms and legs were frozen in place. I could only scream, but there was no one to hear me. I screamed again and a shadowy figure came from the trees.

I couldn't be sure if the figure was real or not. It sort of resembled Adam, but I could see it was not Adam. The figure walked over to me and stretched out something like the long things that Adam had on both sides of him and touched me. I grabbed the shadowy figure and squeezed with all my strength.

I heard a voice, "take in a deep breath through your mouth and then push like you do when you're getting the berries out" I did.

One huge sensation was so unbearable I stopped being aware of anything. It was just like the times when there was no light and Adam and I lay under the bushes or in the hole in the hill waiting for the next light. Then I heard a voice saying. "You have a baby boy, hold out your arms and I will put him in your hands" I heard the figure speaking before my eyes could clearly focus. Something was in the figure's hands, and he was extending his arms to me. I don't know how I knew what arms and hands were but when the figure spoke to me, I understood.

"What?" I heard the words coming from my mouth. "What is a baby boy?" I asked again as the baby was given to me. I looked at the new "baby." I looked from the baby to the figure and back at the baby with questions that I could not ask. The animals had many little animals with them, but the little ones looked just like the large ones only smaller. This "baby" didn't look anything like Adam or me.

The figure stayed with me until the light went behind the trees and came back the next day. "I will stay with you. I'll teach you how to care for the baby. You will be the only one able to see or hear me. I won't leave you. You are my assignment. I'm going to teach you everything that you need to know."

Adam found me in the plants as soon as the sun was in the sky. "What is that?" he asked as soon as he saw me and the baby.

"A baby," was the first answer that I gave Adam. Then I said, "With the help of the Lord I have brought forth a man." (Genesis 4:1, NIV). Adam looked at the two of us for a very long time. He did not go to pick berries that day or the next. The shadowy figure stayed with me, but I knew that Adam did not see him. I named the baby Cain meaning "I acquired him from the Lord."

After Cain was born, my shadowy figure stayed with me constantly until Abel was born. When Cain cried, he would tell me what to do for him. He ran through the plants with Cain and me because Adam was away finding berries and green plants that we could eat. Cain had been with me many days when my middle started to grow again. The shadowy figure told me that I was going to have another baby. He promised to stay with me and help.

After Abel was born I could call and see the figure, but now I had to call out. I didn't call out in my speaking voice, it was more of a thought or a quiet whisper. When I called, the figure would come and help me. As the boys grew the figure was present but only showed up occasionally. I could see that my boys were very different as they grew to the size of Adam.

Both boys had grown to Adam's size, and they often stayed away from Adam and me for many days before returning. One day the shadowy figure just appeared. I was surprised because I couldn't remember the last time I had seen the figure.

"I'm glad to see you. It's been a long time since you showed yourself to me?" I said to the figure as Adam came running to where I was standing. I remembered that only I could see the figure.

"Adam, why are you running?"

"Cain. It's Cain." Adam called out to me between gulps of air to fill his lungs.

"What about Cain?" I asked.

Adam said, "I started back from the field where the berries and plants that we eat grow. Birds kept flying over a spot at the edge of that field. I tried to chase them away, but they would fly off for a few minutes and then come right back." He stopped talking and took in a long gulp of air then continued, "I walked closer and saw what looked like a stick poking out of the ground. I pulled on the stick and Abel's dead body was under the dirt. Cain put him there!"

"Ohhhh! Help me." I called to my shadowy figure. My heart ripped in my chest as Adam's voice pierced my ears. I just screamed, "Ohhhh! Help me."

My shadowy figure stayed beside me as I walked the three steps between Adam and me to hold out my arms to him. Adam leaned over so that his head touched my shoulder before his body began to shake. We stood fixed in that moment, the full weight and reality of our lives clearly before us.

"They are gone." Adam said when he stopped shaking. "Cain killed Abel and God banished Cain. They are both gone."

Both of my babies were gone; one to death and one to exile. I would never see either again.

Adam and I never forgot our Cain and Abel, but we had other children after the loss of the first two. We taught the later children what we learned by caring for the first two.

My shadowy figure was always with me, but in the later years I could only sense the presence. It became a very rare occasion when we had an exchange of words. One day I asked what had happened.

"You have grown now. You know me and my ways. It is enough for you to sense my presence. You have learned the meaning of courage through the events of your life. You are able to encourage others because of what I've taught you. I am as much a part of you as your own essence. You have learned to make My thoughts your thoughts so we are in agreement."

I was the first female human, and I was alone. Courage is not a word that was known to me. Life came at me, and I faced it with the strength and tools at my disposal. In my weakest moments I had the strength of my shadowy companion; in my strongest moments I had the fellowship of His presence.

My encouraging words to you, "Aloneness will come with life, embrace it, and live on. Just as the light and dark periods make a day in the cycle of life, so too do the periods of aloneness and comradery make a day in the cycle of life.'

Rebekah: Barren and Misguided

Rebekah is my name. I believe that you've heard a lot about me, and probably have an opinion about the kind of person that I am already. Regardless, I want you to hear my story from me. My father was Bethuel, the Aramean. My grandfather, Nabor, and Abraham were brothers. My brother, Laban, and I grew up in Paddam Aram. Laban and I heard our father speak of our great-uncle Abraham and his possessions, but we never saw him. In the stories that we heard, great-uncle Abraham left Ur to follow God and traveled to the land of the Canaanites. He had great wealth, at least it sounded as if it were great, when Laban and I listened to the stories about him.

When I was old enough to travel alone, I went to the springs every afternoon with the other young girls to get water for our family and water the camels. We carried large clay jars on our shoulders for the water. It was easy going down to the springs with the empty jar, but it took time to learn to balance a full jar of water on your shoulders; then climb back up from the springs. When I was a little girl, I could only carry half a jar, but by the time I was fifteen I could carry a full jar.

Before the stranger came, my life was very ordinary and routine. Mornings were for baking and cleaning the camel pens. Afternoons were for watering the camels and bringing water back from the springs for the family. Sometimes at the end of the day, when the camels had been watered and fed, Laban and I would talk. He would tell me what the others in our father's household talked about.

"The boys think that you are very beautiful," he would tell me. They say, "A camel driver on one of the caravans is going to steal you, and I won't be able to get you back." He would have a very serious expression on his face just before he broke into an uninhibited laugh that seemed to go on without end. Then we would both begin laughing. Some days I would think of what the boys said on my way to the springs.

On the day that the stranger came, I left for the springs ahead of the other young women. The afternoon overhead sun was still very hot, the desert sand burning to bare feet. About halfway down to the springs I stopped to shake sand from my sandals and adjust them. Walking back up from the springs, with my water jar on my shoulder, I saw the stranger and his camels loaded with packs on their backs standing on the path.

Watching the stranger, my brother's words rang in my ears, "A camel driver on one of the caravans is going to steal you and I won't be able to get you back." Fear filled me and I began shaking so badly that the water jar almost fell from my shoulder. It lasted for only a few seconds. Suddenly, my fear was replaced by wanting to talk to the stranger.

Before I could say anything to him he said, "I've been walking a long time. Please give me a little water from your jar."

I couldn't say anything. My hands lowered the jar from my shoulders to give him a drink.

"I'll draw water for your camels too until they have finished drinking," I heard coming from my mouth. I struggled to recognize the person talking with this stranger. It certainly didn't fit anything that I had known about myself to that point. Nor did I recognize the young woman who eagerly turned her face up to the stranger who placed a gold ring in her nose and bracelets on her wrist. The Rebekah who left home just an hour earlier thinking only about getting the family's water would not act in this manner. More amazing and out of character was the answer that I gave to the stranger when he asked to spend the night in our house.

"We have plenty of straw and fodder for the camels, as well as room for you to spend the night." I ran back to tell my brother and father about the stranger and his camels.

Laban went out to the springs to meet him. In a very short time, I saw Laban and the stranger walking toward our tent. Laban and my father and the stranger talked for a long time. I couldn't get close enough to them without being seen to hear what they talked about. The entire household was talking about the stranger and his camels. Soon father and Laban sent for me.

"Rebekah," father looked directly into my eyes. "This is your great-uncle Abraham's servant. He's come to get a wife for Abraham's son Isaac. He told us that he prayed to the Lord to send the right woman to him. You answered everything that he asked of God. Your brother and I have given you to him to be a wife to Isaac."

"A wife to Isaac." The words exploded in my ears. A few hours earlier my only thoughts were of getting water for the family and enjoying a conversation with Laban. Was I hearing correctly? Father and Laban's faces told me nothing, but I knew it was settled, according to Father and Laban. I would leave in the morning to return with great-uncle Abraham's servant. I couldn't sleep that night. My entire life had changed in a day. No longer would great-uncle Abraham be a name only person, in a distant land. He was going to be my father-in-law. I would see all of his possessions for myself. When morning finally arrived, my nurse and maids were ready to leave with the servant.

Mother and Laban stopped us before we could go out to the servant. They said to him, "Can't you stay and visit a little longer? Give us ten more days with her."

"Send me on my way," he said to them. "Now that I've completed what my master has asked me to do, I must return to my master."

Mother and Laban were not willing to let me go. They tried one more ploy to delay our departure. "Rebekah," I heard mother's voice calling me.

"Do you want to go with this man?" Mother asked as Laban watched me.

"Yes." There was no other answer for me. I had spent the entire night imagining what my life would be like in this new place married to great-uncle Abraham's son. Uncle Abraham was known all over the region. Travelers on the caravans talked about him. Some even claimed that they had met him or lived near him. He was famous. What other answer could there be but "yes"?

Riding a camel is hard work. I had to balance myself and adjust to the rocking back and forth as the camel walked. The desert was hot during the day and cold at night. I could not allow my nurse, or any of the maids that father had sent with me, to see fear in me. No matter how tired I was at the end of the day's travel, I would not let them see me cry or pamper my aching body. When the torches were out with only moonlight to fill the night sky, I allowed myself to rub my sore parts, hidden by the dark of night and blankets that kept the desert night cold at bay. Days later I looked out across the desert and saw a man coming in our direction.

"Who is that?" I asked the servant riding on the camel just in front of me. My veil lay across my lap. I reached for it to cover my face as the man approached.

"That's my master, Isaac," he answered as Isaac approached. The servant rode out to meet him and they returned to where I, face covered with veil, sat on my camel.

"You are very beautiful," Isaac told me when he removed my veil, after we entered his mother's tent. It was our first night together. I wanted to tell him that he was handsome like my brother Laban, but the words wouldn't come out. My eyes saw the age lines that the desert wind and sun had etched into his face. I looked closely. He was much older than I, looking more like my father than my brother. Yet, this was my husband. I looked forward to my first sign that I would give him a son.

Deborah, my nurse from childhood tried to comfort me after the first three months when I was still not showing any signs of a son on the way. "I will hold your son," she'd say to me after each time there were no signs of my being with child. It was months, then years, twenty in all before I changed.

Isaac talked to his father, Abraham, about the child that he did not have until Abraham joined his fathers. Each time I overheard one of their conversations, my spirit became increasingly dejected. Everybody knew about the covenant between Abraham and God.

"How could Abraham be the father of a great nation if his son, Isaac, didn't have even one child?" The more I heard about the covenant, the worse I felt.

Isaac saw my grief and my weight loss. He tried to encourage me, but each time I looked for signs of a child and found none, I sank a little lower. Finally, one day after years of disappointment, I just let it go. I remember I was sitting in the tent thinking about my childless state and all of the disappointment that I felt. I remembered the other women looking at me with pity in their eyes. I felt my own hopelessness. In that moment I can't tell you what, but I felt something deep within just break. I stood up and called for my maid.

"Bring me some fresh water," I said to her. "Lay out my new robes. I'm putting on everything new. I will not wear any of this old stuff again. I'm going to stop trying to give Isaac a son. I will just live out my life and enjoy every day that I have. I don't know who will give Isaac a son. If love is all that I can give him, then that is what I'll give him."

I enjoyed six of the best weeks of my life. I felt light and carefree on the inside. I looked for something new every day. Deborah and the maids noticed the change in me and started to bring me things that they found in the desert to add to my collection of "new life things." Isaac started spending more time in my tent at night before going to his own.

One moment it was there and then, just as quickly as it had come, it was gone. My mornings turned into torture. I couldn't stand the smell of smoke from the morning fires, or the meat for breakfast roasting on them. My body felt as if it were being torn apart from the inside out. Deborah noticed the change in me first, then the maids, and finally Isaac.

No one spoke to me of my second great change. Isaac didn't have his dad to talk with anymore so we sat in my tent, each of us trapped in our own silence. I wanted to tell Isaac that the long-awaited son was on the way, but I was afraid to speak. I don't know what Isaac thought because we sat in a surreal peace. As we sat, he would look at me and the furrows in his brows seemed less etched. Even after my body changed so that there was no denying my growing belly, we did not speak of the child.

After one particularly hard night of what felt like war within my growing belly I screamed out to God. "What is happening to me?"

"Two nations are in your womb and two peoples from within you will be separated; one people will be stronger than the other, and the older will serve the younger." (Genesis 25:23 NIV). An audible voice spoke to me in the darkness. Terrified. I lay trembling in my bedding. Abraham and Isaac often talked about God in their conversations. They never said he talked to them like another human being. Slowly my heart pumped softly enough for me to stop hearing the pounding in my ears. My body stopped the uncontrollable shaking, and my brain began to think about what I had just heard. His answer shocked me more than I could imagine or believe. What was I supposed to do with that information? "Two nations growing inside my womb." Nothing about those words made any sense to me, but I didn't forget what was said.

Deborah was with me when the time to give birth came. After two days of my having pains, but no birth, the elder midwife was called. She examined me when she arrived and said, "Rebekah, you are having twins."

I remembered God's words, "Two nations."

Esau was born first. His skin was vibrant red, not the pale and subdued color of most babies. He was this bright red and covered in hair, unlike any other baby that I had ever seen. Isaac loved him from the moment that he first saw him.

The second baby, Jacob, was born within minutes of Esau. He was born holding Esau's heel. Jacob was my baby. I loved both my children, but Jacob was my baby. As they grew, Esau was drawn to the fields, but Jacob stayed close to home. Esau loved hunting and would be in the fields all day. He would bring his father animals that Jacob and I would cook in a stew for him. When the stew was ready, Esau would take it to his father. Jacob and I would sit outside the tent. I watched the two of them, Esau and his father. The idea came to me to help Jacob get the oldest child's blessing from his father even though his brother was the oldest. I remembered how just a few weeks earlier Esau had been willing to give his birthright away for a bowl of stew.

The Christian Bible has a full description (Genesis 27:1-46) of what happened so I won't repeat it here. I will say that I had plenty of time to think of how I had helped Jacob cheat his brother. When caravans came from Paddam Aram, I asked of my son. I heard of his marriage to Leah and Rachel and the birth of their children, but I never saw my grandchildren. My husband Isaac was old and wanted to see Jacob's children but died without seeing his grandchildren. I had plenty of time to think about what I'd done after Jacob left us. I often wondered how it might have been if I had not encouraged him to cheat Esau out of his birthright. I knew Esau had made a rash bargain because he was hungry. After Jacob left, I was never sure I had done the right thing in interfering.

What is the encouraging message that you can get from my story? One action based on a rash decision or impulse can forever change the course of your life. I am remembered into eternity, not as a loving wife and mother, but as a conniving woman who plotted with one son to cheat her other son of his birthright. That is not the way I would have wanted to be remembered, but it is the way that I am immortalized in the Protestant Bible.

Leah: Unloved and Rejected

*H*ello, my name is Leah. If you attend church or listen to sermons, you've probably heard and possibly read about me many, many times. I wonder if you've ever thought about me, about what my life may have been like. If you've heard sermons about me, they generally focus on my being the oldest daughter of Laban. In most of those sermons, I'm portrayed as the daughter who was forced on a man who didn't want her, but wanted to marry her younger sister. That's all true. Today I want you to hear my story from my own mouth in my own words.

Courage, encouragement, encouraging, what is that? I spent my childhood days playing with the camp children until I was old enough to help the women. When I started helping the women, it sounded as if they were talking in code about the smell of the men when they came to the tent at night. They used words that I did not understand while at the same time moving their bodies around in circles without moving their feet. I wanted to ask questions, but I was afraid to ask any questions. Questioning was not allowed.

I was six years old. One morning after I had heard my mother screaming most of the night, she called me into her tent. "Look Leelee," she said to me while unfolding the blanket that she held in her arms.

"She's a girl, so you'll have someone to play with now," my mother whispered to me so that the other women and servants wouldn't hear. "Isn't she pretty?" My mother pulled the cover off the baby's tiny face so that I could see. I was very happy when my mother sent for me to see her new baby, my little sister.

Pretty was a new word and meant nothing to me until the other girls started telling me that Rachel, my little sister, was pretty. My mother, nor anyone in the camp, had ever called me pretty. I would look in the camels drinking trough to see my face, but it just looked like my face. Inside I knew that pretty meant something that Rachel had but I did not.

During my entire childhood, our father never spoke to me unless it was to tell me about some other work that I needed to do. Rachel could make him laugh with her stories, but he didn't have time to listen to me. When I was fourteen, Father said to me, "Leah, I don't know how I'm going to get you married before Rachel. The boys remember what you looked like before you grew up enough to start wearing your veil." Then he just laughed.

It was just a few months later when the stranger, Jacob, came from Beersheba. He caused great excitement in our camp. He said that he was our father's sister's son.

On the day that he came, Rachel ran into the camp exclaiming about his strength. "Leah" exploded from her mouth at the same time that she gulped in a breath of air. "He just rolled the stone that it takes two shepherds to move, away as if it was nothing." She gulped in another breath before continuing. "When the shepherds arrived at the spring all of my sheep had been watered because he helped me draw water for them." She wouldn't stop talking about the man.

After he came to camp, I saw how he followed Rachel around. He had been with us seven years when Father announced to everyone that we were going to have a wedding. I wanted to ask Father who was getting married, but questions were not allowed. When the camp heard that a wedding was about to take place, the women all began to gather around Rachel. Everyone had seen how Jacob followed Rachel around. I wasn't invited to the "women" talks with Rachael.

It was very noisy and loud the night of the wedding feast. All attention was on Rachel. I stayed on the edge of the campfire circle. Suddenly, I felt a hand over my mouth and someone pulling me backward. I couldn't scream, but I was terrified. I knew that the men would drink too much at night and if they wanted one of the young virgins, they would just snatch them away. I was dragged far enough away from the campfire that my calling for help couldn't be heard over the noise and commotion. The person holding me turned me around.

"Father!?" My mind went blank. I couldn't think.

"Shh!" Father said removing his hand from my mouth just enough for me to gasp a breath. "Listen to me and do exactly as I say." He paused, looking at me intently in the moonlight. "Go into the marriage tent and get under the covers before anyone can see you. Give your veil and cloak to Bilhah before you go in. Tell her to go and sit in your place at the feast."

Father was giving me to Jacob as his wife. Everyone in the camp knew how Jacob had been following Rachel around for the last seven years. He had barely looked at me even when walking directly past me. Father wasn't thinking about me. He was only concerned about what it would look like to the tribe for his youngest daughter to be married before the oldest. I walked as slowly as I could to the marriage tent. I waited for one of the unpredictable sandstorms to blow up and take me away as I'd seen it do a young goat or calf, but nothing happened. The night was quiet and the desert wind cold. Only the bright glow of moonlight and distant sounds of men drinking too much wine and women dancing because another virgin would join the ranks of women tonight shrouded me.

Bilhah, my faithful friend since I could remember, followed me from my tent to the marriage tent. Shame washed over me as I removed my garments to get into the bed of a man who expected someone else. She took my clothing piece by piece and dressed in them as I did what my father had instructed.

I waited, lying as stiff as I could, not knowing what to expect and expecting nothing. Finally, in the early hours of the morning he came into the tent. He smelled of sheep and cattle and wine. Nothing was said that I could understand, only mumbling in a drunken slur. The desert night air was cold as he lifted the covers to lie beside me. I felt hard rough hands on my body. I willed my mind to hide me in a sandstorm where nothing could be seen and only the scrubbing sand could be felt. The heavy tent fabric that had protected me from sun and rain, sand and locus swarms, and bone chilling cold, could not keep out the soul chilling cold slowly engulfing me. Father had found a way to get me married before Rachel.

"Jacob, Jacob." I spoke close to his ear to wake him for his breakfast.

"You're not Rachel!" he spat the words at me when he heard my voice. "You're not Rachel!" His disgust palpable as his words filled the space between us. "You're not Rachel," he said with the sound of his voice sinking deeper within him. He sat quiet and motionless, elbows on his knees with his bowed head held by his upturned hands. He looked like someone who has lost the only thing that they ever cared about. "You're not Rachel," he spat the words out of his mouth as if he had just tasted rotten goat meat as he stood, pulled his woolen robe around him, walked out of the tent, and joined the camp for breakfast.

Zilpah, one of Father's other maidservants was waiting outside the tent when I pulled the tent flap back to let in the sunlight. "Zilpah, what are you doing here? Where's Bilhah?" came out of my mouth in a rushing stream of barely audible words. I fought to hold onto what I could of the life I had known.

"Your Father gave her to Rachael," she said walking into the tent from where she had been waiting outside with water for me to wash. I washed and scrubbed myself, but no matter how hard I scrubbed I could not get the smell or feel of him off my body.

Everybody in the camp knew what had happened, and not a person spoke to me when I joined the women for breakfast. That week was unspeakable. I knew my husband was coming to my tent just so that he could have my younger sister for his wife. Yet I had to endure his coming. I was now one of the married women. I could sit in their circle when they made bread and wove wool into garments. I didn't talk. What could I tell them? My husband didn't love me. His touch was rough and uncaring. He wouldn't wash to come to me. I couldn't get the smell of the sheep and cattle out of my nose. He came to me on the last day of my bridal week after butchering sheep for Rachel's wedding feast. He still had dried blood on his hands when he reached for me.

He didn't come back to my tent after he married Rachel.

Zilpah told me that Bilhah had said, "He only comes to you when he can't be with Rachel because of her monthly uncleanness."

He even stopped doing that when he saw my growing belly. He didn't ask about the baby or me. He just stopped coming to me. Zilpah and one of the other maids helped me when it was time for the baby to be born. Zilpah became my only friend. I suspect it was because she felt sorry for me. She heard the camp talk and laughing.

I named the baby Reuben. Jacob looked at the baby, but I couldn't tell how he felt about him. Such was my life. My husband would only come to me when my sister Rachel was unavailable to him. I bore him two more sons, Simeon, and Levi.

I named my firstborn Reuben because it means God has seen my misery. I thought giving my husband a son would change his feelings toward me, but it did not. I named my second born Simeon because God knew that my husband did not love me and gave me a second son to increase my stature in the community. I clung to the hope that my husband would love me. After my third son, Levi, was born I said, "Now at last my husband will become attached to me." How wrong I was.

Zilpah, my three children, and I remained in the camp, but apart. I couldn't leave because I had nowhere to go, so I endured the stares and looks. I pretended not to hear the women laughing and talking about me. I held tightly to the fact of my three children. I had something that Rachel, even though she was jealous, could not take away from me. Every time my husband had come to me, I bore him a son. He stayed with her, except during her monthly time of uncleanness, but she bore no children. I hoped that my children would bring him to me, but when I stopped conceiving. Jacob just completely stopped coming to me, I asked Zilpah about the camp rumors.

"Rachel gave him Bilhah," she answered me in a matter-of-fact tone. "And Bilhah is going to have a baby for Rachael."

After being with Rachel and Bilhah there was nothing left. Rachel bragged about winning her struggle with me when Bilhah gave birth to a second son.

She was my sister. I had no struggle with her. It was our father's doing that gave me to Jacob instead of her. I was not responsible for Jacob's having to work another seven years for her, but I was blamed in her imagined struggle.

Two could play the "give your husband your maid for a wife scheme." So, I made Zilpah go to Jacob as his wife. Yes, that hurt to make my only friend go to my husband, but Rachel forced me to put her in that position.

Jacob did nothing to refuse Zilpah. That made my hurt all the greater. Zilpah bore two sons for Jacob, Gad, and Asher. I thought that I could finally hear the women call me happy. That did not happen. Everything that I desired was beyond my reach. I had given my husband five children, three that I bore, two that my maid bore, and still his heart had not turned to me.

At my lowest point I bought a night with my husband from my sister. My son had gathered some mandrake plants for me. I used those mandrake plants to pay my sister for one night with Jacob. Yes, I said that I was at my lowest, or so I thought.

That evening I stood on the path from the fields to see my husband on his way to my sister's tent. "Jacob, I have bought you for tonight. I paid Rachel for you with the mandrake plants that Reuben gave to me." He said nothing, not even raising he eyes to look in my direction, but after dark he came to my tent.

God gave me a fifth son, Issachar, because I gave my maidservant, Zilpah, to my husband. I still hoped that my husband would change his heart toward me. I gave birth to Zebulun, my sixth son, and still no honor came to me. Jacob loved Rachel and not me. He always returned to Rachel as soon as her uncleanness was finished. Dinah, my daughter, was the last child that I bore to Jacob. I came to accept my position. I was unloved by my husband. Nothing would change that.

We left my father's tribe in secret after Dinah was born. Jacob didn't tell anyone in the camp that he was leaving. One night he gathered all his belongings, people and animals and left in the quiet and darkness of night. My father did not get to say goodbye to his grandchildren or me.

We traveled about ten days before my father and his men caught up with us. We had camped so that the children and young animals could rest. Fear for my young children gripped me. I wanted to go outside when I heard the voices of Jacob's men shouting. I stayed in my tent with my arms around the children. The shouting outside grew louder and suddenly stopped.

I released my children and made my trembling legs and feet walk to the tent flap. It took seconds that seemed like hours to raise my hand and open that flap. I didn't know what lay on the other side, but I was prepared to see Jacob or Father or both on the desert sand with blood covering their bodies. My hand reflexively grasped my mouth to stop whatever sound trying to escape my lips.

Jacob and Father stood in the middle of the tent circle shaking hands with each other. My father and Jacob made peace, an oath to each other, and a vow before God that neither would try to harm the other. When I heard the words that they spoke to each other, I knew that I would never see my father again. He and his men rode toward the horizon behind us. Jacob and his men broke our camp and again started traveling. I was going to a place that I didn't know to live with a people that I didn't know. I only had my children and Zilpah. Jacob cared nothing for me, proving that later on when we met his brother Esau.

My husband was afraid of his brother. He knew he had cheated him when they were both at home with their father and mother. I had heard Jacob talking to his men about what happened between he and Esau. He feared his brother would still be angry with him and kill him, so he devised a plan to send his family in groups to meet Esau. He sent Bilhah and Zilpah with their children in the front group. He sent me and my children in the next group and put Rachel and Joseph in the last group. When my husband thought that we all might die he made sure that Rachel would be the last person and the one with the greatest chance to escape.

We were nomads, traveling from place to place. Rachel's time to give birth to her second child came when we were traveling. We all stopped to await the birth. She refused to allow me into her tent. Her midwife came out and said, "She is having a very hard time." I could do nothing.

Hours later the midwife came back to the campfire and said to Jacob, "You have a son." Before any excitement could be expressed, she said, "Rachael is dead."

Jacob came to my tent and placed the baby in my arms without any words exchanged. Halfway to the tent opening he turned and looked at me holding my sister's baby. His eyes looked past me to some distant place. His shoulders dropped and his arms hung limp at his sides. He stood there until his legs began to move toward the tent opening. My life had reached another turning point from which there was no return. Jacob never entered my tent again.

Courage, encouragement, encouraging, yes, I know something about those words and that process. I learned how hard life can be when you need someone to give you encouragement, but none see your need. I learned how loud the silence can be when you want to hear an encouraging word, but all that you hear is blame and an accounting of your shortcomings. I didn't live to see my son, Judah, become the Lion of Judah, nor did I live to see David become king of Judah and Israel. I lived my life unloved and undesired, but Jesus Christ is in the lineage of my son Judah (Matthew 1:16).

What is my message of encouragement or my encouraging word to you today about the bad relationships in your life? The love and acceptance that you seek, and desire will come to you through God working in your life to fulfill His plans and purposes. You can only see today with your natural eyes. You must allow your spiritual eyes to gaze upon Jesus Christ and see the future that is coming into being because God loves you. God is aware of every relationship, and he is working in each one.

Hannah: Challenged, and Ostracized

Hello. My name is Hannah. I am Samuel's mother. You may have knowledge of me or not. Many sermons have been preached about my prayer for a son, my vow to give him back to God, his birth, and my follow through on my vow. The book of I Samuel in the Protestant Bible recounts the incident of my meeting with the priest, Eli. That is not the story I'm sharing today. What I'm sharing with you today is the story of my life prior to that trip to Shiloh for the annual sacrifice. Today I am telling you about my family and the Anointing that operated in my life: how it allowed me to endure Peninnah's provocation and the freedom that I gained when I received an answer from the Lord.

After marriage, my family included Elkanah, my husband, his wife Peninnah and their children, and the servants. In the beginning I did not understand anointing. I learned about anointing as I lived with Elkanah, Peninnah, and their children. Peninnah taught me what it means to be anointed and how the anointing works to bring us to God's purpose for our lives. Elkanah was married to Peninnah when he asked my father for me as his wife. She was older than I and already had two boys. In the second year of my marriage, she gave birth to a third child, a girl. The girl was two when the family was preparing for the annual trip to Shiloh for the sacrifice. She sat on my lap as I combed her hair.

Peninnah came across the camp to where I sat and said, "Here darling. Come to Mommie," as she extended her arms to the child. "We don't want Hannah's 'condition' to rub off on you so that you won't be able to give your husband sons to carry on his name." Her voice increased in volume with each word so that by the end she could be heard by the entire camp. "Maybe she'll get better by the time we go to Shiloh next year," she said, looking directly into my eyes just before swirling away from me to walk off clutching the baby to her chest.

I sat stunned, unable to move until she was on the other side of camp, too far for me to run after her. My shame began to creep up the sides of my neck as I felt the hot blood fill the small veins in my neck then my face. The color on my cheeks announced to anyone who cared enough to look above my veil that Peninnah had scored a direct hit to my sense of pride and self-worth. I lived in a culture that valued a woman by her ability to produce a male child for her husband, preferably within the first year of marriage, certainly by the second. Three years of marriage had gone by for me, and I was still unable to produce a child, much less the all-important male child.

Still immobilized by Peninnah's words, I felt the soft pressure of a hand on my shoulder before I heard the voice.

"Hannah?" It was the soft assured voice that had comforted me so often after one of Peninnah's outbursts. "I heard what she said." He moved his hand from my shoulder to hold my hands in his as he gently massaged my palms. "I can't do anything to make her stop tormenting you. She thinks that I love you and I don't love her." His voice sounded almost apologetic. "It's not true," he continued. "I love her, just not the way that I love you." He broke the loud silence that descended upon the two of us. "Come, let's walk," he said while nudging me from a sitting position with a soft pull on my hands that he still held in his.

The years passed and every evening Peninnah faithfully waited for Elkanah to return from the herds by standing in the opening of one of the front tents. He would accept the bowl of goat's milk curds and the basin of water to refresh his face from her before walking to the center of the camp where the main dinner fire was burning. She would wait to find a seat until he was seated. When he didn't invite her to sit near him, she would choose a spot directly in front of him so that he was always in her line of sight. I sat next to him with an open space between us in which none of the family would sit. After the dinner fire burned down, he would come to my tent unless it was my forbidden time. Then he would go to his tent or if he wanted, he went to Peninnah.

Year after year, she treated me as if I were in competition with her for Elkanah's attention when that was never the case. There were times when I saw her sitting in front of her tent just watching Elkanah. Occasionally she would move her hand to her cheek and wipe. He never saw her because she would quickly go inside the tent if he turned in her direction or started toward the tent. Whenever she saw Elkanah talking to me, she or one of the children needed his attention.

One evening after a very hot summer day when the men had worked extra hard to draw enough water for the animals Elkanah just walked past the tent where Peninnah waited for him. He went straight to the dinner fire and sat. He looked in the direction of the fire for a long time as the maids turned the roasting meat. Finally, he looked across the fire to where Peninnah had seated herself. He raised his hand and motioned for her to come sit with him.

"Hannah," she said when near him. "I'm staying with my husband tonight," her voice in a singing cadence. "See to the maids getting the children settled." Without waiting for an answer from me she sat in an empty space next to Elkanah. He made no effort to acknowledge her.

My sleeping tent was on the opposite side of the camp from Peninnah's which made it easy for me to see when Elkanah went to her tent. Whenever he went to her tent, that was her excuse to send me a message by one of the maids. "Go tell Hannah that Elkanah will be staying with me. I'm sorry that she won't be bringing a new baby with us to Shiloh next year."

Every year the family went to Shiloh to worship and sacrifice to the Lord. The year before Samuel was born, we arrived at Shiloh and began preparation for the sacrifice. Peninnah and I were watching our meat pots as Elkanah divided the meat for each of us.

"Hannah is getting more than her share," Peninnah complained following Elkanah back to the store of meat from which he filled each pot. At the sound of her voice I turned and walked to where they stopped. "She doesn't have any children! Why is she getting more than I get?" She stood in front of Elkanah blocking his view of the pots, forcing his attention to her so that he had to stop and answer her.

"Peninnah you and your children get double what Hannah gets." Towering over her five and a half feet frame Elkanah looked directly down at her and said, "You are correct. She doesn't have any children. That's why she gets more." Silence encased the three of us.

Splash! The loud splashing sound broke the silence. Peninnah stood between me and the pots blocking my view. I looked around her shoulder just in time to see her son throw rocks into the pot of meat.

"Peninnah, your son just threw rocks and dirt into my pot!" I screamed at the top of my lungs. "He just ruined the meat," I managed to gasp out with the last of my adrenaline produced breath.

Elkanah turned and the three of us saw the back of the child's robe disappear around the back of his mother's tent. I stood there sobbing uncontrollably. Peninnah stood silently with a blank expression on her face. Elkanah covered the three paces between us in one step and wrapped his arms around me. "Hannah, what's wrong? Why are you crying?"

The three of us stood there in sight of the meat pots locked in an endless struggle. Peninnah just stood there within reach of Elkanah's arms. He made no effort to reach out to her reinforcing that she was forever outside of the embrace that she desired from him. I stood within the embrace of his arms receiving all that his love could give, yet empty and incomplete inside. In that moment, Elkanah was completely giving of himself to me, but incapable of giving me what he knew I desperately wanted. He could not recount the number of times he heard me speak of my childlessness. I stood within the circle of his arms as long as I could, feeling the shudder of his helplessness and held back tears. He knew that it would do no good to scold Peninnah's son. Scolding could not give me the status of woman in Peninnah's eyes. Only my giving Elkanah a son could do that.

We knew, the three of us, Kilion and his wife, and I, as we stood locked in that endless struggle that I had all of the love that earth could give me. Peninnah knew as she watched Elkanah and me that he could never give her what she desired. Yes, sons and daughters he could give her; she wanted his heart. I had the love for which she longed. He knew it as he poured himself into me to stop the flood of pain pouring out through my eyes. I knew it as I felt his heart breaking for me. I had everything that earth could give me. And in that moment, I knew it would never be enough. With the remaining strength of will left to me, I tore myself away from Elkanah's arms and ran to the Lord's Temple.

I walked back to our camp with my shoulders straight after my visit to the priest with his words ringing in my ear. Our trip home from Shiloh was very different than the past years. Peninnah, who usually made sure that she and her children surrounded Elkanah with no room for me moved to the back of the caravan. I walked behind the lead animals as I had always done. That arrangement left Elkanah to walk alone. As we made our way home, I noticed that Peninnah would not allow her children to taunt me as she had on the trip to Shiloh. Something had changed.

The priest's words replayed themselves in my mind so loudly that I did not realize that I had stopped walking.

"Hannah, Hannah!" I felt my body being shaken as the frightened voice filled my ears. "What is it? You're just standing here in the desert." My eyes focused and I could see the caravan at some distance in front of me. Only Elkanah and I stood there in the desert. "One of the men came to tell me that you had stopped walking and were just standing looking at the horizon." His voice, usually quiet and strong, was trembling and shaking with each word. His face had a worried look that I had never seen before.

Frightened, I quickly repeated to him what the priest had told me. The muscles around his mouth formed a smile that covered his entire face. "Let's go home," he said in the voice that I had grown to expect and love.

I knew that Elkanah had always loved me, but on the trip home from Shiloh I saw a new tenderness and gentleness in him towards me. When we left for Shiloh, I knew that I was loved; now I knew that I was cherished and desired. I could feel the specialness and tenderness with which he treated me. Even the touch of his hand on my shoulder as he helped me with the unpacking when we returned home from Shiloh, spoke a new language of love because the men never helped with household chores. There was no longer a struggle between Peninnah, Elkanah, and me. It wasn't a matter of winning and losing. It was order being established and walking in God's purpose and divine plan.

When I talked to the Lord's priest, I felt something warm and sharp touch my mouth and then travel over my entire body. I was fully alert with my eyes open. Only the priest and I were there. As I prayed and talked with the priest, I had a clear vision of what God had created me for, my life's mission.

The specific job that I had been assigned was made clear. Pain and provocation at the hands of Peninnah over the years had equipped me to complete my assigned task. At God's appointed time, He extended

His hand and touched my mouth. Afterwards I could speak the vision for the specific job that I was created to completed.

It was two years before I returned to Shiloh with the family for the annual sacrifice. The first year away, my baby, Samuel, was too young to travel. The next year he had not been weaned. On the third year I returned to Shiloh to give my baby back to God as I had promised when I talked to the priest.

What did Peninnah teach me about courage, encouraging, encouragement and anointing? First comes the challenges that build character and strength. I needed more than human strength to finally receive the one thing that made me feel complete and then give it back to God. That strength will not come from earthbound love or human sources. Second, God is in control of the timing. At his appointed time, He will reach out His hand and touch your mouth so that you will be able to acknowledge your equipping for the task. You will be able to state a clear vision of the task assigned to you. Finally, you will have a thorough understanding of your specific job. In summary anointing is at God's choosing; it flows one way, from God to man. God extends anointing (His touch) and humans receive anointing (God's touch). The anointing comes with God's speaking His purpose and plans for you. The anointing is the touch of God in appointment for mission.

What can I say to you about encouragement and encouraging? It comes from unlikely sources in unusual circumstances.

Deborah: Uncommon Role Model

*E*ncouraging and encouragement. You want me to tell you something about the whole concept of encouragement? Where do I begin? I lived in Israel after the strong leadership of Joshua and before the kingship of Saul. It is said of those times, "In those days Israel had no king: everyone did as he saw fit." (Judges 17:6 NIV). It was a difficult time, made more so by the frequent failure of Israel to remain true to the covenant between Israel and God.

My name is Deborah. I am a prophetess and leader of Israel, married to Barak Michael Lappidoth. Rabbinic literature, specifically the Midrash, creates a clearer picture of what the Rabbis thought of me than the Christian Bible. Barak was not thought to be a learned man, so I made very strong wicks for the Tabernacle. The wicks that I made gave a brighter light than those made by the other craftsman. My husband took the wicks to the Tabernacle. My vocation was wick maker. The people knew that I made the wicks that Barak brought to the Tabernacle. As a reward for my good deeds (making the wicks for Tabernacle), Torah scholars came to me to learn.

Midrash, The Rabbinic literature, which is an interpretation of Biblical narratives, helps you to understand the meaning of my husband's name. Barak means face like lightening. Michael is either after the angel Michael or because he would lower himself. Only Barak and Lappidoth are listed in the Christian Bible. Midrash writers agree that the word *eshet lapidot* is formed by the root words *lapid* (torch) and *lapidot* (unlearned). I didn't think of my husband in any way other than my husband, the man to whom I was married. That can't be said of the people among whom we lived. They had a very low opinion of Barak.

In the beginning our life was (what you could call) normal for the times in which we lived. Our days consisted of getting food, making the wicks, trips to the Tabernacle to deliver them and the trip home for the evening meal. I knew what the people thought of my husband, but I didn't dwell on that. Things begin to gradually change. As more Torah scholars came to me for teaching, I became more known as a prophetess and woman of wisdom than the wick maker.

I became one of the Judge, leaders of Israel, because people listened to my wisdom and counsel. I regularly encouraged the people to attend Tabernacle and obey God's law that Moses had given to us. My encouraging words did not change the people. As punishment for our sin God sold us into the hands of Jabin, a king of Canaan, because of the evil done in the eyes of the Lord. Jabin ruled and oppressed us for twenty years before the Lord gave me directions to tell Barak to assemble an army to fight Jabin.

My court was located between Ramah and Bethel in the hill country of Ephraim under the Palm of Deborah. The desert weather was not kind as I sat there day after day hearing the same quarrels coming from different people. I knew that the real problem was that the people were no longer obeying the laws of God. They no longer respected the Ten Commandments given to them by God for community order. Yet, I sat and listened to story after story of how someone had made wooden idols and placed them on altars in their homes; pronounced the name of Yahweh in debased language; failed to keep the Sabbath holy; defamed their parents; coveted a neighbor's property and violated a neighbor's wife; killed and murdered; and lied to cover their lawbreaking. One morning after months of crying to the Lord to save us from Jabin, my servant girl and I arrived at the Palm somewhat earlier than our expected time. It was quiet with only the rustling of the palm branches piercing the quiet early morning air. In that stillness as I prayed to the Lord, He spoke to me.

"Go find Barak and tell him to come to me at once," I said to my servant girl putting all of the control that I could summon to keep my voice calm and matter of fact in spite of the excitement that was bubbling up inside of me. "Hurry." I said no longer able to contain my excitement.

She left running to reach the city gate where I told her to look for him among the merchants.

The sun was high overhead when she and Barak returned to the Palm. I quickly excused the people in front of me and walked off to another place where the people would not be able to hear my conversation.

"Barak!" I said, my voice a loud whisper. "This morning after I finished my prayer the Lord told me to tell you that he has heard our prayers! He is going to deliver us from Jabin. You are to lead the army!" Excitement filled me. I waited for his reply. Several agonizing seconds that felt like hours passed before he said, "I can't do this unless you go with me." His hands clutched both of my arms. He looked into my face, his nose inches away from mine.

"WHAT?" God who delivered Israel from Egyptian bondage, provided food in the desert, fought for us and delivered our enemies into our hands has given you a direct message, NO! a direct command, and all that you can say is that you want me to go with you?" The words formed themselves into a sentence in my mind, but I did not allow them to escape my lips. I stood in complete silence looking in my husband's face.

"I need you to go with me." His voice barely above a whisper. "I need you to go with me."

You cannot imagine my shock when I heard him say that he wanted, -no needed- me, to go with him. I knew we needed to be delivered from the ruthless rule of Jabin. So, I agreed to go with Barak. However, it did sadden me to also tell him he would not get credit for killing Jabin because he needed me to accompany him. The credit for killing Jaban would go to a woman.

Barak was my husband and I wanted him to have status as a man of courage and valor in our community. He merited a portion in the World to Come (Rabbinic literature) because of my influence, but I wanted him to merit a portion because of who he was. Barak was successful in destroying Jabin's army but Jael, another woman, was responsible for the death of Jabin. When the battle was over and Israel delivered, we wrote and sang what is known as Deborah's Song (Judges 5:1-31).

My life was not without critics and those who attempted to prevent me from completing any task that I started. One group of Israelites accused me of being guilty of the sin of pride. According to their understanding it was the sin of pride that led to the loss of my gift of prophecy.

Encouraging and encouragement. During the twenty years that I led Israel as ruling Judge encouraging came from my personal knowledge that I was following the laws of God. I was encouraging the people to attend Tabernacle and obey God's laws. Yes, knowing that the Torah scholars came to me to learn was an encouragement. I did not allow discouraging thoughts to remain on my mind when someone made disparaging statements about my husband's unlearned status. I forced myself to think of how faithful my husband was in carrying the wicks to Tabernacle every day. It was personally very discouraging when my husband said that he could not follow God's directions unless I went with him. My encouragement came from my determination to focus on the deliverance of Israel from the oppression of Jabin. I gained courage from the knowledge that Israel would once again be free.

Naomi: Woman Acquainted with Grief

My name is Naomi from Bethlehem in Judah. I lived in Judah during the time of the Judges. That was the time after the Tribes of Israel had been given their assigned inheritance in the land of Canaan. Joshua and the generation that conquered much of the land had died and the next generations had made homes for themselves in the land. You have heard of me in the biblical book of Ruth. I believe that you may have already formed ideas about me and my life. Today I will tell you about my life, and the woman that I was before death visited my family. I didn't consider my life as outstandingly courageous before death visited. Truthfully, I still don't. I just made the best decision for me from the information that I had at the time.

When the Judges led Israel there were times of peace when we just lived out ordinary days. Our routines consisted of getting up when the sun first touched the night sky, working in the fields, spinning lamb's wool into fabric, preparing food, caring for the young and the very old, going to the barter market, and going to bed when the sun no longer shone in the sky above. There were times of war when our neighbors on all sides would try to destroy us. According to the older ones the wars had been going on between Israel and Moab, our closest neighbor, from the time Israel first entered Canaan.

Moab had easy access to Judea by using the King's Highway. It ran north and southeast of the Dead Sea to Bethlehem on the west side of the Dead Sea. The elders told us that when times of war came the

Moabites would use the King's Highway to enter Judea and plunder all of the crops, take the livestock, and destroy as much of our village as they wanted. There was always fear that the Moabites would come across the Jordan river, at the northern end of the Dead Sea, to kill people, destroy crops, and steal anything of value.

Some of the elders attended "The Assembly of the Lord" regularly. They tried to get the people to obey the laws of Yahweh. The elders told the stories of how they had been led out of Egyptian slavery by Moses and all the other history of Jacob's children and grandchildren, but the people soon forgot what Yahweh had done. As soon as they forgot, they began following the Canaanite ways.

I was born just after one of the wars. There was very little food left, only what people had been able to hide form the Moabite raiding parties. One day I was outside playing when I saw Mother and Granny walking across the yard with stalks of grain sticking out their cloaks.

"Moms!" I jumped up and ran to meet them. "Where did you get them? Where did the stalks come from?" I could barely make myself stop jumping because new grain meant fresh warm bread for supper.

"Shush!" Mother said and pulled me closer to her. "Come inside and I'll tell you. I guess that you're old enough to know now." She kept her arm around me as we walked the few steps to the cooking area. "We went to the hill caves. That's where we hide the food so that the raiding parties can't find it. One of the village women stays there to keep watch. When someone comes near, she starts to wail and howl like an animal. That way the person passing won't know that the small animals that we depend on are inside." She stood looking into my eyes. "You must not talk about this. Not even to your friends. Do you understand?" She took her hands off my shoulders as I very slowly nodded my head up and down.

The caves were away from the center of the village so the raiding parties did not find them. My mother and grandmother were able to save enough for our family to get another start with barley and wheat after the war ended. We were able to just get by for a while. My father would come from "The Assembly of the Lord" and tell us about other families that were not making enough for them to live. Sometimes he would tell us about a family that had moved across the Jordan into Moab because of the good fertile ground for growing barley and wheat.

My mother did not go to "The Assembly of the Lord" but after pleading with her, she allowed me to walk with my father. I couldn't go in with my father, so I stayed near the entrance and played with the other children. We could hear the chants and readings. All 13-year-old boys were required to attend and start reading. All the children knew the readings from listening but only the boys were permitted inside and required to read.

The girls stayed outside with the younger children. Elimelech, an 18-year-old from the family that owned a herd of camels, came out before his father, to take his younger sister and brother home. He tried to make the lead camel kneel so that both children could get into the basket on the camel's back. The camel knelt long enough for Elimelech to put his little brother into the basket. Before he could help his sister completely into the basket the camel started biting at Elimelech which made him lose the reins, and the camel ran free. Before anyone could do anything, the camel was running with his brother in the basket and his sister hanging onto the basket rim. Our screaming brought the men running outside.

They came outside just in time to see the camel run right past us with the little girl holding onto the side of the riding basket. The men started running and calling to the camel. Before they could catch the camel it just stopped. A sudden dead stop. The abrupt stop threw the children forward and over the camel's head onto the ground. Men, still running to catch the camel screamed at the scene creating itself in front of them. They couldn't get to the camel before it stomped the children. That is a picture that I could never erase from my memory.

Everything stopped; men stopped running, children stopped screaming, birds stopped chirping, and the camel stopped stomping. I could not take my eyes away from Elimelech. He stood motionless, face fixed on the pile of mangled flesh that only minutes before had been his little sister and brother. His arms hung at his sides as if being pulled to the ground by some invisible force against which he was helpless. No sounds came from him, and the only sign of life in his body was the single tear streak that made its way down his colorless face.

His father stood immobilized between the pile of flesh that had been his children and the son who was still his child. After an eternity his father walked to him and pulled him close. Neither said anything. The younger clung to the older. The older refused to allow the younger to pull away.

I stood watching until the pain growing in my chest became unbearable. That's when I heard a strange voice that I knew must be mine, pierce the deadly silence with a soul shattering nameless sound. Suspended motion reclaimed its rightful place and suddenly there was chaos. Elimelech and his father ran to the children. Some of the men ran to catch the camel, grazing in a nearby field. Children ran home to their mothers. Levites ran out to the mangled bodies on the ground. I ran to a tree and collapsed under its branches where my mother found me.

It was two years later after my 15th birthday before I returned to the courtyard outside "The Assembly of The Lord." Life had moved on after the children were buried, yet almost nothing was changed when I arrived. Toddlers and children played in the yard as their fathers went inside. The older female teenagers stayed in the yard to watch the younger children. One thing was different, one of the fathers also stayed outside to watch the animals. I tried not to look at the place where the camel had stomped the children, but my eye was drawn there by the shadow of a man.

He turned in my direction just as I made my eyes focus on the tree that had been my haven two years earlier. It was Elimelech only not the Elimelech that I remembered. This one was taller and had skin browned by working in the fields. His eyes were deep in their sockets and darted from side to side as if looking for something, but unable to find the thing sought. Watching him walk in my direction the images that I had fought so hard to erase from my mind came flooding back. My body began to shake. By the time that he reached me I did not think that I could stand.

"Naomi?" His voice was deep, the sound of a man but not a man as old as my father. "I wondered if you would come back. Most of the women don't come. They just send the older girls to watch the little ones."

Elimelech thought of me as a woman. That was a subject that I hadn't given any thought. His presence had some kind of calming effect because as he stood close, I could feel my muscles gain some strength. Most of the shaking stopped. We talked about everything except the day that the camel ran wild until it was time for him to go inside. My mother said, "that's nice" when I told her that I had seen Elimelech in the courtyard.

Elimelech and I had been married for 18 years when the raiders came again. Granny had crossed over and slept with her fathers. My mother and I hid food and the animals in the caves as she and my grandmother had years before. The raiders didn't get our seed, but that year a drought came, and nothing planted grew. We made it for another two years, but then Elimelech told me that we had to leave.

"No Elimelech, we can't leave! My mother will be here alone. She won't get to see her grandsons. We can make it. Yahweh will allow the rains to come again!" He wouldn't listen to anything that I said so we packed our clothing, the last of the bread and water, and a few grains of barley and wheat and headed to Moab. Elimelech had heard some men on a caravan talking about the green fields in Moab so he decided that he could go to our enemies for fields to grow grain.

My sons, Mahlon the 19-year-old and Kilion the 17-year-old, were quiet along most of the journey to Moab. When they spoke, it was to ask me if I needed to rest or wanted water to drink. They were not in agreement with our moving to Moab for food, but they respected their father too much to talk to him about their doubts. I had my own doubts. We were willingly walking to the people who had tried for years to destroy all of our people. How would we be received? Would we be able to find land to grow wheat and barley? What about my sons? Would they be able to find wives who would adhere to Yahweh's teachings? What was going to happen to my mother? She had no food, and now that her grandsons were gone, she had no one to help her. All of the people left in the village knew her and would do their best to take care of her, but they had their own families. We walked for days and just as the last of the bread was eaten, we saw the first village. I tried one more time to get Elimelech to return home. It was no use.

The boys and I walked on in silence. I felt a veil slip down and make itself comfortable over my shoulders. I could only send Yahweh a silent distress message.

The Moab village people looked at us with unbelieving eyes when we boldly walked into the village center. I walked with a boldness that I didn't feel but knew that I had to believe. The first night we slept outside the gate in shifts. One of us watched as the other three slept. The boys didn't want me to take a turn, but I felt that it was only fair. I used my watch time to pray to Yahweh. By the end of the first week a Moabite who had a field close to the village told us that he had been watching. He offered us a place to sleep in the stall with his sheep. He gave us our first meal that was cooked for humans to eat. I can't describe to you how utterly hungry I was and how good that clean food tasted.

After about a month, the Moabite allowed us to build a lean-to on his property. He also told Elimelech that he could plant a small portion of his field. After the lean-to was up, we stopped sleeping in shifts. The Moabite had a feast for us and invited his friends. We didn't have a place for the family men to attend worship so we said prayers in our lean-to. It took us two years to get a permanent shelter built near our field. We were eating every day, but my mind was on mother. We had been in Moab three years, Mahlon and Kilion had both married Moabite women, and we had harvested our first crop for market. That's when the stranger came into the village.

We first saw the stranger sitting under a tree in the center of the square. Fear covered me. Although I had begun to trust the village people, I was still not totally comfortable with the Moabites. I remembered the stories that my mother and grandmother had told me about the wars. This stranger brought up all of those memories. My fear was confirmed when we heard that he had asked for us by name. The Moabite on whose land we lived offered to go with us to the village to meet the stranger. Mahlon and Kilion wanted to go with us, so we all entered the village center with the Moabite. Men on the street bowed as we walked by. I knew that it was for the Moabite and not for us.

"Are you Naomi of Bethlehem?" He asked.

"Yes. And these are my sons and my husband." The fear that I felt made me want to surround myself with family and strong men.

"I've just come from Bethlehem and the elders asked me to bring you this." He pulled a small box from under his cloak and offered it to me.

Puzzled, I took the box and held it for some time before opening. I looked into the box and felt the air leave my body. The box contained the comb that my mother always wore in her hair, two plain gold wedding bands, and the dried flowers that I knew she kept from my marriage ceremony.

There was nothing for me to go back to in Bethlehem now. I waited in Moab for my daughters-in-law to tell me that I would soon be a grandmother, but those words never came. Instead, when we had been in Moab for eight years Mahlon came running into our house one very hot summer day to tell me that Elimelech had just fallen over in the field. Earlier that morning I tried to tell him to wait until it was cooler, but he ignored me as was his custom.

Following Elimelech's death, the boys took over the field. A few months later they made the house large enough for them and their wives to move in with me. We were getting along well and looking forward to the next planting. Mahlon brought some fish for our supper to celebrate. We were all sitting around the table enjoying a conversation when Mahlon jumped up and grabbed his throat. "Fish bone."

He started coughing and gagging as he staggered around the table before collapsing onto a chair. "Let me see, MOVE" Mahlon's wife shouted as she made her way to him. "Open your mouth," she told him as she tried to pry his mouth open. "Let me see if I can see it." She poked her finger into his mouth to pull the bone out. "I can't feel anything," she choked out between sobs as tears covered her face.

I stood fixed to the spot. "Yahweh HELP!" I heard in my head, but no sound escaped my lips. The bone didn't come out. Mahlon slid to the floor still holding his neck as the color faded from his face. He thrashed around the floor for seconds that seemed like hours and finally was quiet. His quietness made way for the sound of grief wailing that had not been heard in my ears since Elimelech. His wife stayed with us after he was gone.

The days passed slowly as we adjusted to being three women with one man to look after us. We slowly developed a new routine. Mahlon's widow and I went to the field to help Kilion with field work. His wife stayed home to take care of the house and prepare food for us to eat. About two months after Mahlon died, Kilion's wife told me she thought that she was with child. She and I decided to keep the news between us until, she was sure.

"Naomi, it's not so." His wife said later that month as the three women of the house sat at the supper table. I lowered my head to stop the flow of tears. A baby would have brought so much life and joy back into the family.

Mahlon's widow looked from one to the other of us. "What's wrong? Why are you crying?" She asked looking straight in my direction with a questioning expression on her face.

"Another loss," I said returning her look. "We thought that Kilion might be a father in the spring. But it's not so." I answered in my 'life will go on voice'.

The four of us, Kilion and his wife, Mahlon's widow, and I tried to keep up with the fields and the house. Time for the fall harvest neared. Daily checking for the amount of grain confirmed what our eyes had already told us. There was not enough grain for both selling and feeding us. That night the three of us were quiet as we walked home from the field to wait for supper.

"Supper is ready." Kilion's wife, with her soft melodic voice announced shortly after we arrived. Her voice had a soothing effect that I had not noticed before when she spoke to Mahlon's widow and me as we sat just inside the door.

"Where is Kilion?" His wife asked when she saw that he wasn't with us.

"His lying down," I said. "He wasn't feeling well when we came in from the field today. He said that he'd rest before supper."

"I'll go get him. He wasn't in a good mood when he got up this morning." She said over her shoulder as she turned to go into the house.

Noooo! The ear-piercing scream shattered the night and scraped every nerve that the minutes earlier soothing voice had touched. The ear shattering heart piercing scream filled the house, flowed to the yard outside and wafted into the countryside.

I did not move from my seat. It was not necessary for me to confirm what my heart had already told me when the scream reached my ears. I had come to Moab to survive a famine. It was now complete. Moab had taken everything that I held dear, my mother, Elimelech, Mahlon, and now, Kilion.

I was alone in a strange land that I had tried to call home. My companions now were my two widowed daughters-in-law and Grief. Grief was a persistent and unwelcome companion.

Weeks after Kilion died, caravan travelers brought news that the famine was over in Judah. After a sleepless night, my decision was clear. I was now 48 years old, no parents, husband, sons, or grandsons. Alone and with only two Moabite daughters-in-law, it was time for me to return to Judah the land of my fathers.

My life to that point had been hard. I lived between the highs of marriage to Elimelech, the birth of our sons, and the lows of our journey to Moab, the death of my mother, followed by the deaths of my husband and sons. Yes, the life that I lived was hard with spots of brightness. It had enough pain to sustain the grief. Did I have courage? From where did I receive encouragement? Is there anything that I can tell you about courage, encouraging, and encouragement? I can only tell you that I faced and lived each day. Yahweh's presence and laws were ever present and with me and my life depended on them.

Orpah: Culturally Bound Messenger of Hope

Hello, my name is Orpah. I'm Naomi's daughter-in-law who returned to Moab at her insistence. The Bible narrative stops at the tearful goodbye between Naomi, Ruth, and me, but my story doesn't end there. That is the beginning of a life that I would have never expected or imagined as I grew to adulthood in Moab.

Elimelech, Naomi, Mahlon and Kilion came to Moab at the height of the famine in Judea. Everybody in our village was afraid of the Israelites when the family came, but the meager food that they had been able to get during the famine had rendered them gaunt and frail looking. There was nothing frightening or imposing about this family. They just looked like people in need of food. They settled into the life of the village and soon Elimelech found work. When his son asked my father for me as a wife, I was a little nervous but more excited than nervous. The Israelites had customs different than the ones that the Moabites practiced, especially when it came to the gods. They had one God; we Moabites had many.

The first year after my marriage, we stayed with my husband's parents. I learned how to make all of the different dishes that were served at each of the sacrifice days. Naomi, that's my mother-in-law, was distant at first. She would often ask me why I wanted to learn about Israelite meals and sacrifices.

"I want to be a good wife to my husband, he's an Israelite. You don't do as we do here in Moab," I would always answer as I stopped whatever we were doing and looked in her direction.

Finally, she stopped asking, and just answered my questions or showed me what she was doing. After two years of marriage without any signs of a baby on the way I gathered enough courage to ask her about it.

"God gives the babies," she answered without taking her hand away from the spindle that she was using to create new bed covers. "You have to pray to God like Rachel did to get a baby." We were both quiet for a long time.

"I don't know how to pray to your God," I finally offered, my voice just above a whisper. My hands were shaking so hard that I could barely hold the bed covers.

She stopped stuffing the cover and dropped it to the floor. Looking directly at me she found my tear-filled eyes with hers. Then she walked around the spindle to where I stood with feet nailed to the floor.

"Come," she said as she placed an arm around my shoulder and motioned me to sit on the bench near the spindle. "I'll teach you how to pray to the God of Abraham, Isaac, and Jacob." Her voice had a tone and quality that I had never heard before that moment. I sat there and allowed every word that she spoke to enter my being. I can't explain what happened, but I had never felt anything like the feeling that came over my body as Naomi prayed.

When my husband came home from the fields that afternoon, I told him about the prayer his mother had prayed for me. I waited for him to say something, but he just looked at me in silence. I didn't tell him that I had memorized every word of the prayer. I can't tell you how I did that, but I prayed the same prayer over and over.

Naomi and I never spoke of that prayer again. Occasionally, I would notice her looking at me, then turn away when she realized that

I had seen her watching me. The years went by. I didn't see any results from my prayer, but I continued to pray. I added some new words, and even made up a new prayer of my own. I made sure that no one from my Moabite family knew that I was praying to Naomi's God.

It had not been a happy time when my husband asked my father for me as his wife. Father finally agreed when I told my parents that I was going to marry, even though the man that I wanted to marry was not a Moabite. My insistence came from an unknown place. I would have never defied my father prior to my meeting Naomi and her sons. My stand for marriage made it hard for me to continue as before with my family. My sister told me after the wedding that Mother cried during the entire marriage ceremony even though she did not attend. Father had forbidden her. My husband's family became my anchor. Life went well until it stopped going well.

My father-in-law died. He wasn't sick, didn't have an accident, and wasn't mauled by a forest animal; he just up and died. Before we could recover from his death my husband's brother died just as suddenly. My anchoring family was in a state of shock. I didn't know what to do so I slipped away by myself and prayed. It wasn't the prayer that I had memorized, but one I said as the words came to me. It had been some years since I prayed the memorized prayer. I liked the prayers where the words just came to me better, so I had been praying those prayers whenever I could slip away from my work or my husband.

We, my mother-in-law, sister-in-law, husband, and I, were beginning to pull ourselves out of the deep sorrow into which the death of my father-in-law and brother-in-law had hurled us. Then another blow came to the family. The last male, my husband, died unexpectedly just as the other two men had done. We were alone, three widows with few supplies and few prospects for replenishing. My mother-in-law, Naomi, announced that we were going back to her homeland in Judea because we were destitute, and it only looked to get worse the longer we stayed in Moab. The famine had been broken in Judea and there was plenty of food.

There was no time for me to say goodbye to any of my Moab family, since we started the journey back to Judea before the sun was up the following day. We walked in silence, the only sound being the rustling of the robes we wore. By sunrise the village where we had lived was just an outline against the horizon to our backs. Two days later in midmorning Naomi stopped to rest under a desert palm tree with its sparse shade. She took one of the raisin cakes that we had prepared for our journey out of the basket and offered it to me. The night before she gave one to my sister-in-law and me. We ate in silence. I didn't want to say anything. My world was changing faster than I could sort things and find my way. Talking didn't seem like the right thing to do. Just then Naomi interrupted my thought.

"Orpah," she called me by name, took a long pause, inhaled deeply, and began to speak again. As soon as I heard her call my name my heart began to beat faster. I could not remember the last time that I had heard her call me by my name. She would just begin talking when we were in the same place, or she would do something to get my attention and then begin talking. She hardly called me by my name.

By the time that "called me by name" encounter and exchange ended, I was alone in the desert. The midmorning sun was beaming its rays of light and heat on my head. I stood under the palm tree with a skin of water and a few raisin cakes, trying to force my feet to begin walking back to a world that I left when I agreed to marry the man from Bethlehem. I wanted to turn and look behind me to see if I could still see my mother-in-law and sister-in-law, but I knew that there was no use. The swishing sound of robes as they walked had long ceased to send sound to my ears.

I stood in the middle of emptiness. Behind me was a world an unknown number of days walking away. That world, Naomi's homeland, I didn't know and had been told that I could not enter. Two and a half days walk back to where I just left was a world I had said goodbye to years earlier. To the right and left lay the unknown, no road, not even a trail, suggested that I could find my way to what lay beyond the horizon that I could see. I was alone so there was no need for me to pray in silence or attempt to hide my prayer. I prayed to the God of Abraham, Isaac, and Jacob because He had become my God. The Moabite gods of my youth no longer filled my spirit after Naomi taught me to pray. No longer did I think of the gods of the Moabites as gods for me.

I had listened for years to the stories that Naomi told about the way that God had talked to Abraham. I heard how Isaac had wandered and God had finally given him rest. I heard about Jacob and his wrestling with the angel all night. Naomi would tell these stories to herself.

One day I asked her about the stories. She said to me, "It's so that I don't forget who God is. I don't want to forget what He has done for the Children of Israel. That's why we celebrate the feasts, so we don't forget."

We never talked about her stories again. I learned them by listening to her when she was working and talking to herself. One night after we finished celebrating one of the feasts I slipped outside and prayed to Abraham's God. I asked him if he would take me as one of the Children of Israel since I was married to one. There wasn't any kind of answer that I could hear, but all of a sudden, I had a different feeling come over me. It was unlike anything that I had ever experienced. I stayed outside until my husband came looking for me to see if I were okay.

That day standing under that desert palm, I prayed. The sun seemed to get hotter. I looked up at the sky and overhead there was a small cluster of clouds. Something about the clouds captured my attention and imagination.

As those clouds moved across the sky it looked as if they arranged themselves in the outline of the village wall where I had lived as a child with my parents. As soon as I recognized the outline the clouds would stop. Next the formation would disperse and reform in the shape of the house where I had lived with my husband and his family. The clouds repeated that forming and reforming pattern several times, each time a little closer to the horizon and a little further away from the palm tree where I stood trying to figure out the overhead display.

I don't remember when I started walking retracing my steps on the path to follow the clouds. My aching shoulders and neck told me that I had been walking and looking up at the clouds for some time. The palm tree was barely more than an outline on the horizon behind me. On the distant horizon in front of me I could see the clouds. Night came and, in the moonlight, I could see a cluster of palms. I can't tell you why I wasn't afraid, but I didn't feel alone. The following evening when I began to feel hungry, I looked up to see the cloud formations and they had dispersed. I had no more raisin cakes and water. Tears began to well in my eyes. I stopped walking and started to pray. Overhead a screaming bird forced me to open my eyes. On the horizon in front of me I could barely see what looked like an outline of buildings. I started walking again.

Night came and I was standing in front of my parent's house. The journey back to my childhood home convinced me that I needed to tell my family about Naomi's God.

I can't tell you about courage. I can only tell you when my mother-in-law bid me goodbye under that desert palm tree it seemed as if my world had ended. I wanted to lie under that palm tree until the sun burned the life from my body and the birds of the air had a new meal. A force that I did not recognize arose within me and said "Get up. Go. Your life's work is in front of you."

I began to walk following the clouds in the sky. Was that courage? Were the clouds encouraging?

The sun was hot, the sand burning, still I walked. Each step carried me toward a known unknown. My feet could not stop even when

I wanted them to do so. Cloud formations pulled me forward as if I were tethered to them. A faint outline of the village wall grew more distinct with each step. The magnitude of the unknown also grew with each step. Certainty of my task failed to diminish the enormity of what lay in front of me. Did courage lead me forward? From whom would I seek encouragement? Without the support of spoken words and assurance of continual human comfort I walked forward with the certain knowledge that I was not alone.

In truth my life was just beginning. I spent the remainder of my time in the earth realm living and sharing the story of Naomi's God with a people who had a desperate need for him but no knowledge of Him.

Bilhah: Property of the Master

My name is Bilhah. I was given to Rachel by her father, Laban, when she married Jacob. My life is divided into two distinct phases which I call "BR (before Rachel) and AR (after Rachel)." My "BR" life began when I was born into Laban's household. My mother and father belonged to him. We were not the only family that belonged to Laban. All of the workers, including herdsman, skilled craftsman, gardeners, and anyone needed to keep the household operating smoothly, belonged to Laban. When not moving, the household lived in many tents that covered the desert landscape. When it moved, the caravan seemed to stretch from horizon to horizon. There were a lot of people, both adults and children that made up the household. Laban's family, his wife and children, were the center around which everything else revolved. Everybody had a place. All of the "owned people" knew that their place was to maintain the existence and status of Laban's family.

My earliest memories include big groups of children all playing together in the desert sand. Some adults played with the children and others watched for the sudden dust storms and stray animals that would attack the smaller children. As we played, one of the many dust storms started. Suddenly, all play stopped, and adults started rushing the children to form a circle, hold hands, squat, and put our heads on our knees until the storm stopped, if we were too far from the Children's tent to go inside. We had to remain squatting together in the huddle until the dust stopped blowing. Sometimes it would be a few minutes and sometimes it would be hours. When the storms lasted more than a few minutes the household men would carry us to the Children's tent. That's where the weaned household children, except Laban's, stayed until they were old enough to start working with the adults. The weaned children slept in the Children's tent unless their parents came to get them for the night which did happen occasionally. Laban's children had their own tent with maidservants to care for them.

I was six years old when I made my first trip with my mother and her sister to Laban's tent. My mother and her sister were Laban's wife's maidservants. The tent was very large with things spread out around the tent floor, not like our small tent where everything was just in the middle. At night my mother and father pulled the pillows and rugs out of the stack and spread them out on the floor of the tent for them and the nursing baby to sleep. During the day my parents' tent was empty because every adult was working somewhere, and the children were in the Children's tent.

Laban's tent had rugs and pillows in different stacks in different areas of the tent. During the day, the maidservants would help Laban's wife with dressing and combing her hair before they brought her food. Once I was old enough to start work, my job was to go to the big trough outside the tent, fill a basin with water and bring it to my mother for Laban's wife's use. As I grew and was able to take on larger jobs, my duties changed. I helped with the cooking, gardening, gathering the fowls, and keeping Laban's wife and daughters' clothes clean and mended. By the time that I was twelve, Laban's wife started sending me on errands to the sheep shearers. I would carry water and bring back wool for the women to spin the fleece into wool for garments.

I was fifteen when I started into Laban's tent early one morning. Just as I was about to enter the tent, as I had done every morning for the last year, the sound of a male voice stopped my hand that was about to pull the tent flap back.

"She is old enough to marry, but there is no one who wants to marry her." I recognized the voice as Laban's. I heard enough to know that he was talking about his daughter Leah.

"There is someone who wants to marry her," his wife's voice was raised above the quiet soft voice that she always used when speaking to me or my mother or aunt. "You don't want her to marry him because of his father. The boy would make a good husband, but because his father is one of the younger shepherds and doesn't have anything to give you, you are refusing to give her to him." Her voice trailed off and the air was silent.

My hand moved involuntarily and returned to its hanging position at my side. I backed away from the tent as quietly as I could, hoping that my robes did not make a rustling sound. My mind was racing with what I had just overheard. The rumors that had been going around the entire household must be true.

The women were saying, "What a shame. Leah deserves a good husband." The men were saying to each other, "You ask him for her for your son. He likes you," only to hear "No the new shepherd's son follows her around wherever she goes. He wants her for a wife."

Leah was Laban's older daughter and we had formed as much of a friendship as was possible between the master's child and a servant's child. Leah was kind to me. When her mother sent me to help her spin lamb's fleece, she gave me the smaller spindle and pile of wool. When she stopped spinning to get water, she would take me with her. I liked working for Leah. Several times she told me stories about one of the household boys. We both laughed about it until we had to stop the spinning. I grew to be Leah's maid without anyone formally assigning me that job. It grew out of our friendship.

Rachel, Leah's younger sister, burst in on us during one of our spinning and laughing sessions. She had been running and could not talk for a few seconds. Leah and I looked at each other until Rachel began speaking.

"Leah, come quick," Rachel said to her sister while ignoring me. "Our near relative, Jacob, has come to visit. He rolled the stone away so I could water the sheep." She paused to take a breath and started pulling Leah away from her spinning.

Rachel did not look in my direction. She pulled Leah away with her. I followed because a stranger, even a relative, was cause for a household celebration.

All the household members joined in welcoming Jacob. The children had a chance to sleep in the tents with their parents for several nights as the feast continued. At the end of the welcoming feast everyone knew that Jacob would be staying for seven years. He made an agreement with Laban to work for seven years in exchange for Rachel as his wife.

In the time that followed, I felt the not too subtle whispers about my friend Leah that stopped as soon as we approached a group. It was a shameful event for the younger daughter of the family to marry before the oldest. Laban had agreed to put Leah in that shameful position. I became very protective of her even though she was older than I and "owned" me. The next seven years may have gone by fast for some, but they dragged out for Leah and me. We grew closer and shared our secrets about the boys, who were now young men, of the household. All but two of our age had started families of their own. Leah and I were left to ourselves. The household attention was on Rachel and the near celebration of her marriage to Jacob.

The day of the wedding celebration was full of dancing, eating, and wedding games. Leah started out in the morning joining in the festivities, but by afternoon retreated to her tent. I stayed with her until night when she went to the barn fire and sat in the circle. I could see her from where I stood inside her tent. I saw one of the camp men approach her from behind, clasp his hand over her mouth and pull her away from the circle. Panic rose in my throat to scream but before I could speak, I recognized her father's robes in the moonlight.

"What is going on?" I thought. I didn't like the feeling in my stomach. I waited as she and her father walked away from the group at the fire. They were too far away for me to hear what was being said, so I watched until I saw Leah turn toward her tent. Each step seemed slower than the previous until she stood in front of me.

She tried to keep her face turned away from me, but I stood in front of her so that she had to look at me. We said nothing to each other, but her eyes were red, and tears had made a streak as they traveled down her face to drop to the desert sand. We stood looking at each other with thousands of words passing between us in the silence. There was no need for words to tell each other that our lives had just been forever changed by whatever her father had said to her. We stood there in the silence until her father called her name in a loud whisper. She slipped off her robe and veil handing them to me.

"Put these on and go sit at my place in the circle," she said with a voice that was barely above a whisper. She gathered her night attire. With very slow steps she walked away from me in the direction of the marriage tent.

I didn't see her the next morning. I did see her father. "Bilhah," for the first time in my life he addressed me by name. "I'm giving you to Rachel." His words hit me like one of the sudden dust storms. I kept standing where I was. My owner was talking to me. My choice was to listen and do as told, or risk being sold to one of the caravans at best or be beaten to death at worst.

"I sent Leah to Jacob last night. He is angry." Her father was speaking to me again. "I gave him Rachel today. Now I'm giving you to her." With those few words my "BR life" ended and the "AR existence" began.

After Leah's bridal week, Laban gave Rachel to Jacob. Rachel was jubilant. She had the husband that she waited seven years to claim. He loved her and was the total content of her life and talk. I was in the terrible position of seeing the only friend that I had getting what was left of Jacob's time and attention.

After Jacob married Rachel, he did not go near Leah's tent. I could not go to comfort her because Laban had given Zilpah to her as a maidservant. We followed the order of the household. Laban's wife and female relatives had one or two maidservants assigned to them. There was no crossing the lines. I was forced to watch from a distance as Leah tried to make sense of her new life. Rachel was now my responsibility.

Both Rachel and Leah had been married for three months when Zilpah met me at the well one morning. "Leah sent me to tell you that she's with child," Zilpah told me after making sure that no one saw her talking to me.

"Rachel's not," I confided to Zilpah. "She's not going to be happy about this." We left the well without saying that we would be meeting again but we both understood that we would. We continued our well meetings repeatedly over the next eight years. We even stopped trying to keep them a secret. Each time that Rachel heard Leah was with child, and she was not, she became angrier than before.

After Leah's fourth child, Judah, was born, Rachel was out of control with anger and jealously. That's when she pulled me into the middle of her one-sided war with Leah.

"I want a child," she screamed at Jacob when he entered the tent. "Leah has four and you haven't given me any. You don't love her, but you've given her four sons." The one-sided tirade progressed into a two-sided fight between them. "I want you to give me a child!"

I had been inside the tent with Rachel when the tantrum started, but I had heard enough. Just a few feet to my left was the tent flap and my way of escape. I started moving toward the opening when I heard Rachel's voice.

"Here, take Bilhah! Lie with her so she can have a child for me!" All motion in the tent stopped.

"NO!" screamed in my head, but no sound came out of my mouth. I belonged to Rachel, and she could do whatever she wanted with me.

This despicable thing that just came out of her mouth was the last bit of insult that she could heap on Leah. It was almost impossible for me to believe what I had just heard, even though it was a very common practice. I just did not expect to be caught in that situation.

"Say No Jacob! Say you won't do what she wants," formed as an idea in my head that would not exit my mouth as a sentence. I took one look at him and knew that he would not say no. He always gave her what she wanted. This time would be no different. I was just another piece of property to be used to give Rachel what she wanted. Jacob started walking the few steps across the tent to where I stood transfixed, unable to move. He stopped in front of me and the person that I had known my entire life died. A stranger that I did not like from the moment that I met her took the place once occupied by the person that I had been in my "BR" life.

There was no courage, encouraging, or encouragement in betraying my friend Leah, only survival. A maidservant or manservant did not have the right of refusal, only the option to survive. Ours were the arms, legs, and backs that carried the master's children, property, and treasures. We did all of the menial work that kept the household prosperous and functional. We were in sight but invisible, our feet silently gliding across the desert sand when we were moving and making no less disturbance when we were camped. The camp moved on our backs and set up by our hands. Animals were tended by our families for food, clothing, and bartering. Still, we were invisible, in plain sight known only to our own. To those who owned us we were utilitarian property providing everything that sustained the master's household.

One of 300: Invisible in Brightest Light

My name is unimportant now, as it was during the time of Solomon. Just refer to me as "One of the 300". You may call me invisible because I speak for the 300 Concubines attributed to Solomon, who are in reality, invisible. Nameless and without any freedoms, we were kept for the King's pleasure. In seclusion and away from the remainder of the court, our lives were lived out both hoping and dreading hearing the Chief Eunuch call us by name. Girls were collected from all over the territory ruled by Solomon, as well as neighboring regions. Israel enjoyed relative peace during the years of Solomon's reign so there was plenty of time for him to collect us. He had eunuchs whose sole reason for being was to scour the region for young girls to add to the harem of concubines. Many were taken as young as thirteen and fourteen. Most of our stories are the same. This is mine.

"Quick, quick! Get up and sit behind me!" I heard my mother's panicked voice through ears that struggled to return to a wakeful state from a deep sleep the morning after my thirteenth birthday. "Sit up behind me!" she insisted pulling me from the bed to sit behind her as she threw her robe over both of us.

As sleep left me I began to hear the dreaded sound of horse's hooves on the street tearing through the town. Every mother and girl over the age of thirteen both knew and dreaded that sound of hooves beating the road that ran through the center of the village. The King's eunuchs searched the villages, farms, and cities for young girls, some as young as twelve, to add to the harem. There was always one of the eunuchs out among the people whose job it was to watch for young girls. They wanted the girls who were just beginning to look like women but before they had a chance to marry. Families devised elaborate schemes to keep the girls hidden until they were in their mid-teens when they would marry them off to one of the local boys. Marriage and knowing a man were the only things that could save the girls from the King's eunuch.

I sat trembling behind my mother as the sound of the hooves beat grew louder. At first, they were very distant and fast as the horses galloped, then they began to slow. As they grew louder, my heart began to beat faster. I put my arms around my mother's waist and pulled her as tight as my arms allowed. The sound grew louder until it stopped in front of our house.

I could feel the blood pounding at my temple. The robe with which my mother had covered me was made of wool. I felt water form on my brow then run down the sides of my face. Any second the eunuchs would come into the house to carry me off. I felt my legs begin to cramp as I sat with my feet tucked beneath my body. We waited. Footsteps. But they weren't walking toward our door. Slowly the sound faded, and then the horses began to gallop away from our house.

My mother removed the robe that covered us. I felt the rush of warm air touch my sweat-soaked skin. Mother gently prised my hands from around her waist and helped me to stand. Life returned to normal on the street for everyone except the family that lived two doors from us. Their fourteen-year-old daughter was gone probably never to be seen again by her family.

Once a girl was in the hands of the eunuchs she was taken to the court for her preparation. Within a few days of their arrival, the Chief Eunuch examined each girl for suitability. Those found unacceptable for whatever reason by the Chief Eunuch, were returned to their families. Only a few girls were returned to their families after arriving at the court. They were then outcasts because none of the local young men wanted to marry them after they had been carried to the court.

The eunuchs were in charge of the girls day and night. Each girl was told what she could eat, how she was to dress, what her beautification routine would be, even when she was to go to bed and get up. When the King called, the Chief Eunuch selected one of the girls to go to the King. That girl stayed as long as he wanted and then was returned to another part of the palace. Once a girl went in to see him, she could not return to the same sleeping area.

I lived through two more years of near misses with the eunuchs before I was alone at the market and one of the eunuchs saw me. I was a slow developer so that I looked much younger than I was. My mother had gone into a shop for some spice, and I was left alone on the street. She was only gone for a few minutes, but she came back to the King's eunuch holding me by my arm. She dropped the package that she held in her hands and clasped both hands over her mouth. That's the picture that stayed emblazoned in my brain for the remainder of my life. Neither my mother nor I could change my plight. By the time that she could tell my father what had happened, it would be too late for me.

My arrival at the court was matter of fact. I was immediately turned over to the eunuch in charge of the new girls, those not examined by the Chief Eunuch. We were stripped of our clothes and sent to a communal bath. I had not been unclothed in front of another human since my mother stopped dressing me when I was a very young child. I kept my eyes focused on a wall on the other side of the room. My skin turned into a continuous sheet of hives and bumps both from cold and embarrassment. The water was extremely cold when I put my foot on the top step.

"Do you need me to push you in?" I heard a very high-pitched angry sounding voice behind me. "You have until I walk these three steps to you to get into that bath." The slap, slap of sandals on the marble floor made me stumble into the frigid water.

While still in the freezing bath water, the eunuch in charge walked to each girl and cut her hair down to the scalp. I could only scream inside and attempt to stop the tears that freely flowed down my cheeks. "I suggest that you stop that water flowing from your eyes" I heard in that same high-pitched voice. "Get over there and put that robe on. You are holding everybody up."

I pulled the robe as tightly around my body as my shaking hands and fingers would allow. It was a short walk to the Chief Eunuch in another room of the court. We waited as the Chief Eunuch examined each girl. He looked at one of the girls that came in with me and said, "You've been with a man. You cannot go into the king."

It was my turn to stand before the Chief Eunuch. "Pull that robe off." His voice barked at me. Everything about my body began to tremble. "Turn around. I need to see all of you." The Chief Eunuch examined me as I'd seen my father do when he was about to buy a new animal. He probed, pinched, pulled, rubbed, and patted every inch of my body. By the time that he finished the girl that left home with my mother was dead, replaced by someone new. I didn't know the new person and was not sure that I wanted to know her.

The Chief Eunuch looked at the girl who stood a few feet away from me as I tried to cover myself with the robe. "Come here" he snapped in her direction. "Don't stand back there. Come here so I can see you."

I could see her from the corner of my eye. She walked to the Chief Eunuch and just dropped the robe to her feet. "You've been with a man!" He screamed at her. "You can't go into the king". He snapped his fingers together and another eunuch came in to carry her away. So began my life as a concubine.

There were ten of us placed in the new concubines sleeping area when I arrived. We were not allowed to mix with the prepared girls until after our year of preparation. Then we could join the main sleeping porch where we each had our own sleeping area but were free to share space for eating and playing games with the others. The oldest person in the prepared court was twenty-five so she became our "momma." She had been there long enough to get to know the eunuchs and they would bring her bits of gossip and do favors for her. She told us she had never been selected to go into the king and was now past the age to be selected. She would remain in the prepared court unless one of the king's guards wanted her. Then she would be given to him.

There was no set schedule for when a girl would be selected for the king. None of the girls ever came back to tell the others what it was like to go to the king. We lived each day with a generalized fear that we would be selected and never again see the people who had become our friends and "new family."

Courage for me became waking every sunrise to embrace a new day. I knew a second major life change was coming. I just didn't know when it would arrive. Comforting a newly arrived terrified young girl who had been snatched from life with a family that loved and cared for her gave me encouragement. I can add nothing to the story of nameless and countless girls. We share the same story of property used by a man as he desired. Husbands and marriage, No. Children, No. The king's concubines were not known for what was generally accepted as family life. Tears we shed for what was lost never to be regained. New relationships, friends, and reimagined family structure we learned to embrace. Courage and encouragement received and given, perhaps. But life continued and carried us down to our inevitable end. For me, making peace with that end is personal courage and encouraging for others.

Resources

Eve: Groundbreaker and Fountain from Whom all Flow
Genesis 2:4-9; 4:1; Colossians 1:20; I Timothy 2:13

Rebekah: Barren and Misguided
Genesis 23:1-60; 25:19, 23, 28; 27:6, 8

Leah: Unloved and Rejected
Genesis 29:31-35; Malachi 1:3; Matthew 1:6

Hannah: Challenged, and Ostracized
Exodus 29:7; I Samuel 2

Deborah: Uncommon Role Model
Judges 4:1-10, 31; 5:1-31; 17:6; Luke 2:6
Resource. Kadari, Tamar., Midrash Tadshe, Ozar ha-midrashim [ed.eisenstein] 474 in http://jwa.org/encyclopedia/article/deborah-2-midrash-and-aggadah., accessed 26 May 2016.

Naomi: Woman Acquainted with Grief
Ruth 1:1-4; 3:4

Orpah: Culturally Bound Messenger of Hope
Ruth 1:8-14

Bilhah: Property of the Master

One of 300: Invisible in Brightest Light
Genesis 25:1, 6: 30:4, 5 -12: Judges 8:31 Ecclesiastes 2:8; I Chronicles 1:32

Barnabas Publishing, PO Box 2316 Ruston, Louisiana 71272
(318) 514-9724
www.barnabasglobal.net

Publications

Healing Prayers for "Sara Pen"

A collection of prayers written specifically for an individual facing
unique health challenges.
Limited supply. Special Order.
Contact www.barnabasglobal.net for additional information

Praying the Word
Creating and writing scriptural based prayers and
life application principles

Thinking About, Talking To, and Walking with Him Daily
Bible Reading and Study Journal

A Beginner's Bible Study Guide to encourage daily encounters with
the Biblical text and personal spiritual growth.

Pressing Toward The Prize: Pine Trees and Preaching
In his own words, the story of a rural southern ministry couple and
their service over a 60-year span of pastoral ministry.

I Believe: Help My Unbelief
Writings and studies designed to encourage faith practices that
help the reader's personal faith expression when confronted with
overwhelming life challenges.